FOREST ROAD SCHOOL

For Scriveners Ink
H.B.

For Jana
J.O.

First Edition 5   6   7   8   9   10

Library of Congress Cataloging in Publication Data
Buckley, Helen E. Grandmother and I / by Helen Buckley : illustrated by Jan Ormerod.
p.   cm. Summary: A child considers how Grandmother's lap is just right for those times
when lightning is coming in the window or the cat is missing. ISBN 0-688-12531-X. —
ISBN 0-688-12532-8 (lib. bdg.) [1. Grandmothers—Fiction.]   I. Ormerod, Jan, ill.
II. Title.   PZ7.B882Gs   1994   [E]—dc20   93-22937   CIP   AC

GRANDMOTHER
AND I

HELEN E. BUCKLEY • JAN ORMEROD

LOTHROP, LEE & SHEPARD BOOKS   NEW YORK

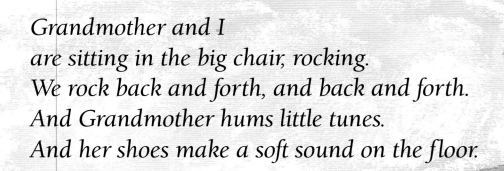

Grandmother and I
are sitting in the big chair, rocking.
We rock back and forth, and back and forth.
And Grandmother hums little tunes.
And her shoes make a soft sound on the floor.

Other people have laps too.
Mothers' laps are good
when there's not enough room on the bus.
Or when you need to have your shoes tied.
And your hair braided.

Fathers' laps are good
when you want to be a cowboy.
Or do tricks.

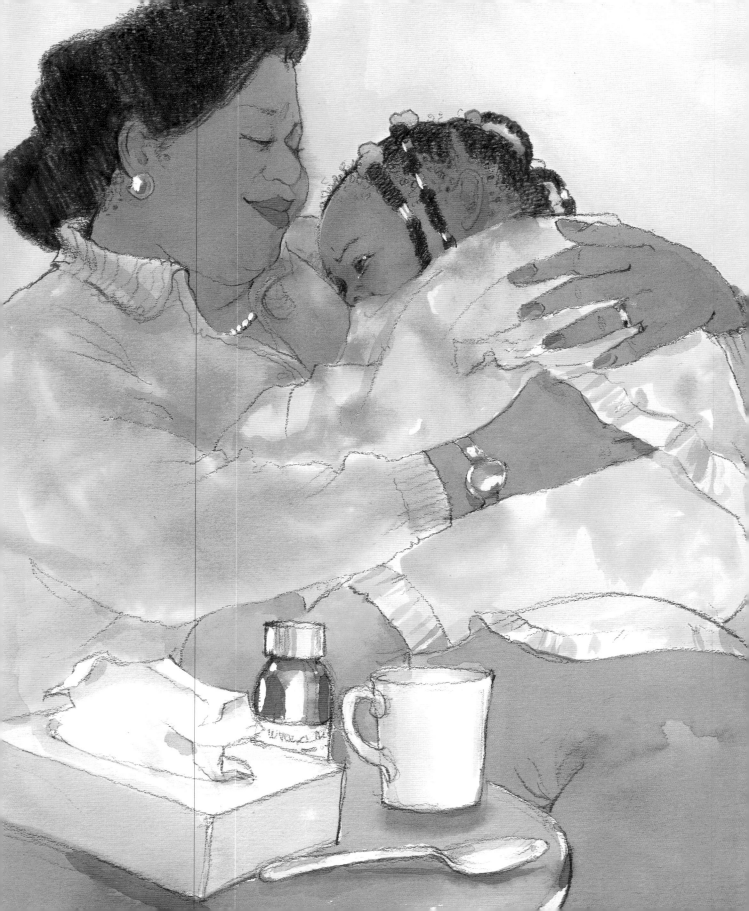

But Grandmother's lap is just right
when you're having a bad cold.
We sit in the big chair
and rock back and forth, and back and forth.
And Grandmother hums little tunes.
And her shoes make a soft sound on the floor.

Brothers and sisters
let you ride
on their backs…

but when they read out loud to you,
*they want you to sit **beside** them.*

But Grandmother's lap is just right
when lightning is coming in the window.
We sit in the big chair
and rock back and forth, and back and forth.
And Grandmother hums little tunes.
And her shoes make a soft sound on the floor.

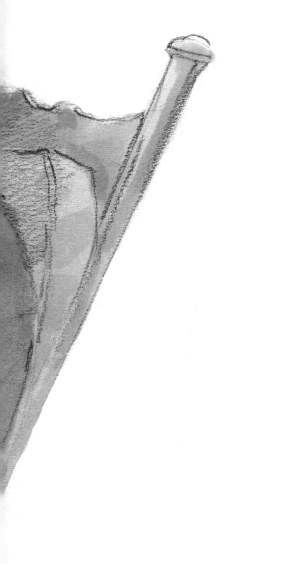

Grandfathers' laps are good
after you've been for a walk.
Or when you want to count the cars
going by.

But Grandmother's lap is just right
when the cat's been gone for two days,
and you don't want to do anything
but sit in the big chair,
and rock back and forth, and back and forth,
while Grandmother hums little tunes.
And her shoes make a soft sound on the floor...

But Grandmother's lap is just right
when the cat's been gone for two days,
and you don't want to do anything
but sit in the big chair,
and rock back and forth, and back and forth,
while Grandmother hums little tunes.
And her shoes make a soft sound on the floor...

make
soft
sounds
on
the
floor.